To my beautiful children,
Russell and Sage.
Together we have learned
to take a slow, big breath.
—S.C.

For Sosi,
my very own peaceful goldfish.
—L.S.

I Am a Peaceful Goldfish

by Shoshana Chaim + Lori Joy Smith

GREYSTONE KIDS
GREYSTONE BOOKS • VANCOUVER / BERKELEY

Sometimes things go wrong.

I have an idea!

I imagine I'm a peaceful goldfish.
I take a slow, big breath in.

Then I let out all my air
to make bubbles in my bowl.

I have an idea, too!
I'm a mighty elephant.
I take a slow, big breath in.

Come on!
I'm a rainbow pinwheel.
I take a slow, big breath in.

Then I let out
all my air to spin
round and round.

Ooh, I'm a
fluffy dandelion.
I take a slow,
big breath in.

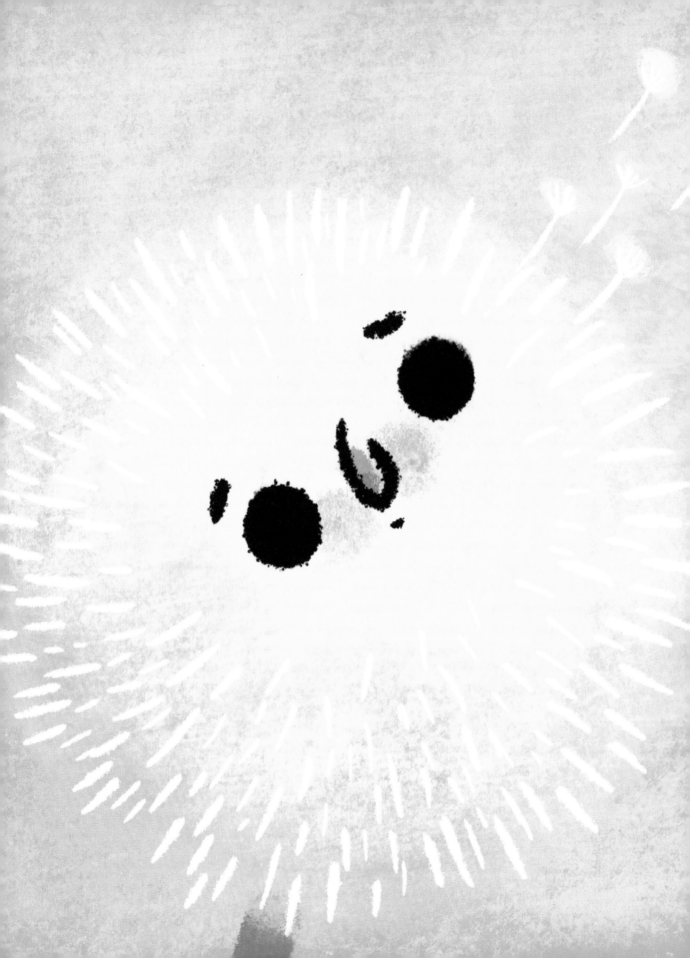

Then I let out all my air
to send my wishes up high.

Look, I'm a
swinging wind chime.

I take a slow,
big breath in.

Then I let out all my air

to make beautiful music.

I know! I'm a gentle dragon.
I take a slow, big breath in.

Then I let out all my air
to make a bright fire.

Now I'm a
growing flower.

I take a slow,
big breath in and
stretch to the sky.

Then I let out all my air

and bring my hands
to my heart.

I am calm.

I am calm, too.

Ready?

Ready!

AUTHOR'S NOTE

Dear little peaceful goldfish,

Sometimes you may feel mad, sad, frustrated, or disappointed. It's okay to feel that way. Do you want to know something? You're not alone, and other kids and adults can feel the same way, too!

Learning to take deep breaths is one of the skills that can make you feel better. When you practice being a dragon, a pinwheel, or a peaceful goldfish, you can remember how to take those deep breaths when you're not feeling your best. Think about some of the animals you love or the activities you like to do. How else can you take a slow, big breath in and let it out? Try it.

Now how do you feel?

Happy breathing!

—Shoshana

Greystone Kids / Greystone Books Ltd.

greystonebooks.com

Cataloguing data available from Library and Archives Canada
ISBN 978-1-77164-637-6 (cloth)
ISBN 978-1-77164-638-3 (epub)

Editing by Kallie George
Copy editing by Paula Ayer
Proofreading by Doeun Rivendell
Jacket and interior design by Sara Gillingham Studio
Printed and bound in Malaysia on ancient-forest-friendly paper by Tien Wah Press.
The illustrations were rendered with an iPencil on an iPad.

Greystone Books gratefully acknowledges the Musqueam, Squamish, and Tsleil-Waututh peoples
on whose land our office is located.

Greystone Books thanks the Canada Council for the Arts, the British Columbia Arts Council,
the Province of British Columbia through the Book Publishing Tax Credit, and the Government
of Canada for supporting our publishing activities.